Pu

Dear Readers,

I apologise for Chester's behaviour in my mouse story. Sorry for the inconvenience.

Sincerely,
Mélanie Watt

Blah! Blah! Blah!

M. Watt

For ~~Marcos, Eva,~~
Melina and Layla For Chester because I
couldn't have made this book
without him. He's the smartest,
most handsome cat in the
world. I wish I could be like
him someday!

First published in Canada by Kids Can Press Ltd in 2007

First published in Great Britain by
HarperCollins Children's Books in 2008

10 9 8 7 6 5 4 3 2 1

ISBN-13: 978-0-00-727018-7

ISBN-10: 0-00-727018-6

Text and illustrations copyright © Mélanie Watt 2007

HarperCollins Children's Books is a division of
HarperCollins Publishers Ltd.

The author/illustrator asserts the moral right to be identified
as the author/illustrator of the work.

A catalogue record for this title is available from the
British Library.

Published by permission of Kids Can Press Ltd, Toronto,
Ontario, Canada. All rights reserved

Author photo by Sophie Gagnon

Visit our website at: www.harpercollinschildrensbooks.co.uk

Printed and bound in Singapore

Chester

NOT Written and illustrated by Mélanie Watt

HarperCollins *Children's Books*

Once upon a time there was a mouse.
He lived in a house in the country.

Then Mouse packed his bags and went on a trip very, very far away and we never saw him ever again!

So Chester moved in
and made a few changes
to HIS new place.

But Mouse returned home.

Oh yes, did I mention he brought back
a really big souvenir with teeth?

Back to the story ...

Once upon a time there was a mouse.

He lived in ... Chester, move out of the way!

... he lived in the country
with his vegetarian dog
who only ate carrots.

Then Mélanie begged
Chester to write a better
story. And it goes something
like this ...

Once upon a time there was ME.
Chester stands for:

Charming
Handsome
Envy of Mouse
Smart
Talented
Envy of Mélanie
Really handsome

Chester lived in Chesterville,
where mice weren't allowed.
It was a beautiful day.

Until it started to rain ...

Now, as I was saying ...

Once upon a time there was a mouse.
He lived in a house in the country.

And he lived happily ever after...

Chester!
This is where I draw the line!

Nope!
I'M drawing
the line!

DO NOT cross this line!

Chester! That's enough!
Hand over the marker this instant!

Chester's busy.

Chester! I'm warning you!
Hand over the marker and apologise
before I count to three!

1...

2...

3 and 4, 5, 6, 7, 8, 9, 10, 11, 12,

13, 14, 15, 16, 17, 18, 19, 20, 21...La! La! La!

All right, Chester!

You want your own story?

You want to be the star of this book?

Well, get ready. Here it is ...

FINALLY!!!

Once upon a time there was a cat named Chester.
He lived in a house in the country.

Chester was a very handsome cat.
Especially when he wore a pink ...

YOU WOULDN'T!!!

NOW it's personal ...